W9-AJG-106

INVASION OF THE UNICORNS

DAVID BIEDRZYCKI

ini Charlesbridge

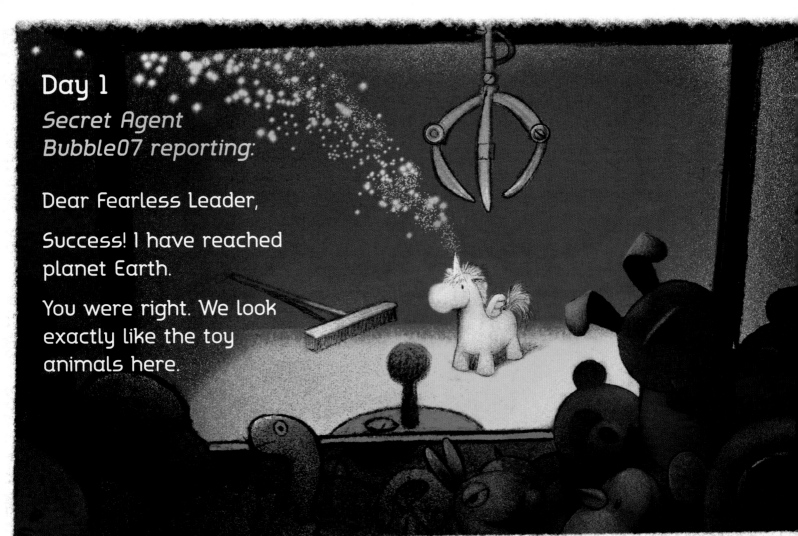

Day 1

*Secret Agent
Bubble07 reporting:*

Dear Fearless Leader,

Success! I have reached planet Earth.

You were right. We look exactly like the toy animals here.

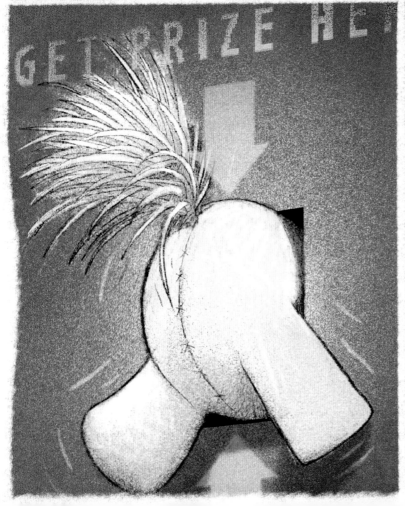

My mission is to decide if our unicorn army should invade this planet and make the Earthlings our humble servants.

First I must allow myself to be captured by an Earthling Family.

This won't be easy.

Their countless attempts to fetch me have not gone well.

I have witnessed what Earthlings call temper tantrums.

Now that my mission has begun,
I must be careful.

Earthling Dog might be onto me.

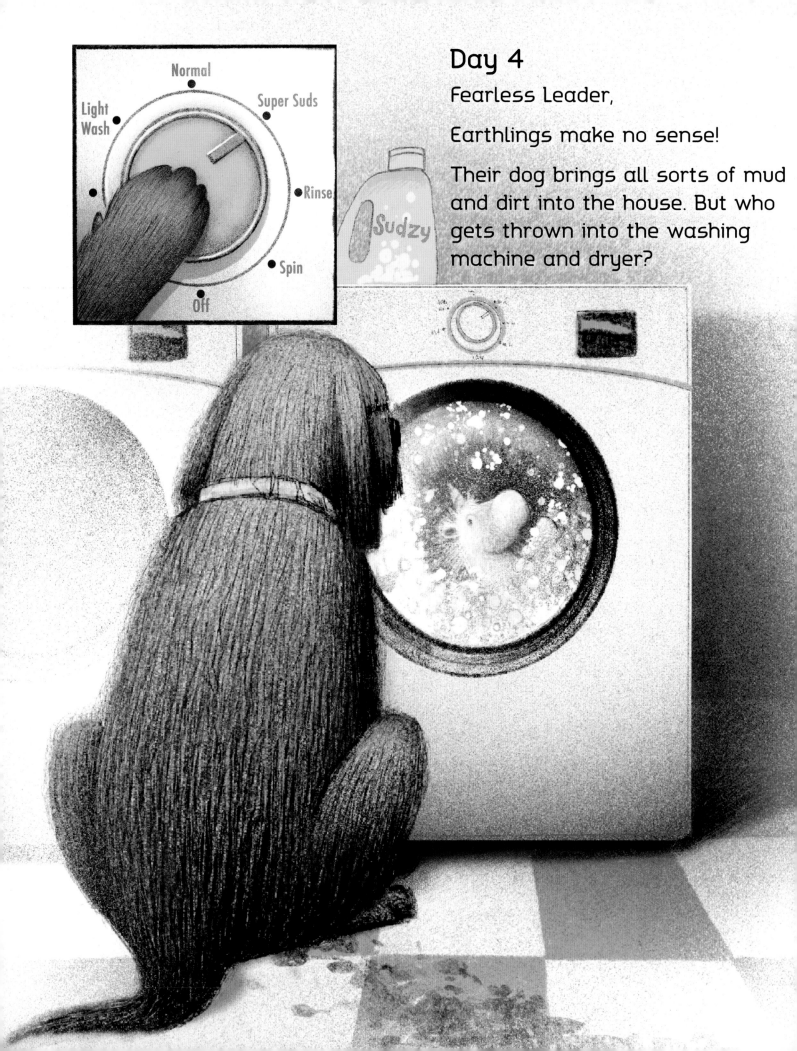

Day 4

Fearless Leader,

Earthlings make no sense!

Their dog brings all sorts of mud and dirt into the house. But who gets thrown into the washing machine and dryer?

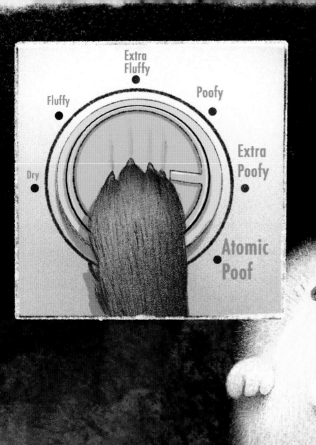

Me.

Day 5

Fearless Leader,

You're not going to believe this!
Every time Earthling Daughter gets
a new toy, she has a tea party.

She loves her toys. She loves them to pieces!

Some are missing their eyeballs.

Is this going to happen to me?

Day 11

Fearless Leader,

Camping is a strange Earthling adventure. Earthlings sit around a fire and eat something called Sa-morrs while they tell scary stories.

And then—get this—
they sleep . . . outside!

I couldn't sleep a wink.

Day 20

Today I rode in a big yellow transport with Earthling Daughter and her friends.

Some of them brought their favorite toys.

Others brought their favorite pets.

And then there were those who forgot to bring their manners.

Fearless Leader, it might be time to invade this hostile planet!

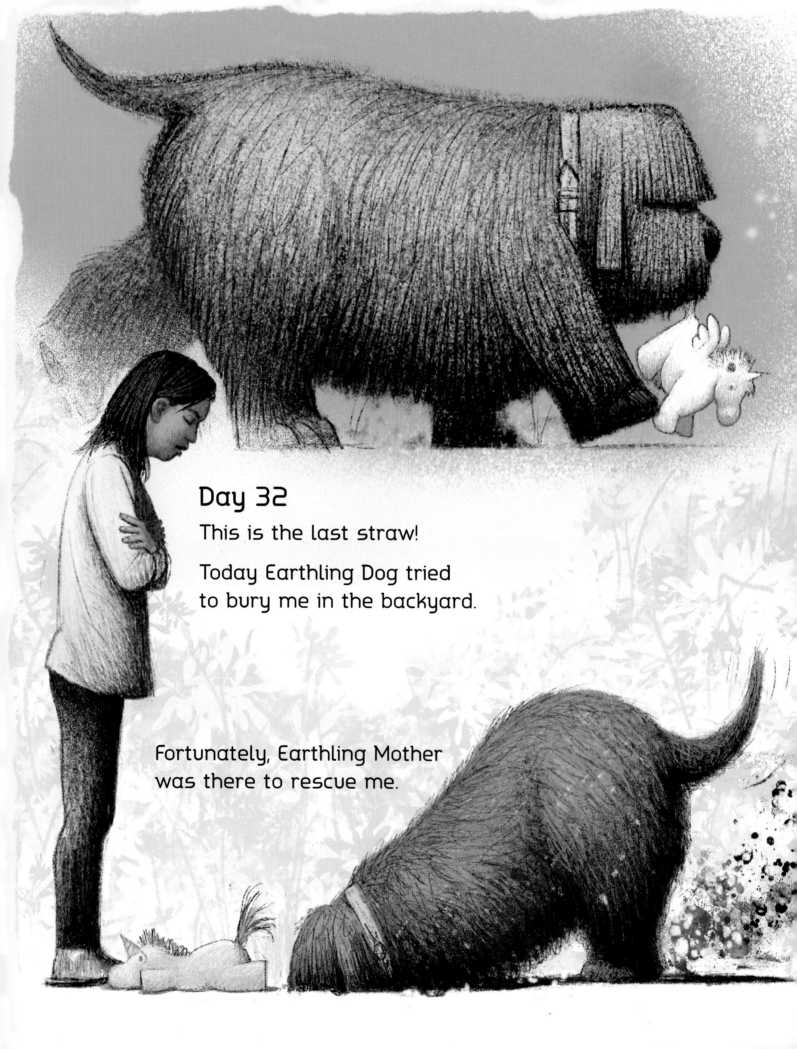

Day 32

This is the last straw!

Today Earthling Dog tried
to bury me in the backyard.

Fortunately, Earthling Mother
was there to rescue me.

Later I got revenge. When everyone was sleeping, I found the most amazing Earthling treat.

Peanut butter cookies!

I left the empty bag next to Earthling Dog.

Fearless Leader, before you come rescue me, I must get this cookie recipe for our planet.

Day 50
Hold off on the rescue! I actually
had some fun. Today was a Snow Day.
There's no school, but there's lots of snow.

Kids eat it . . .

. . . throw it . . .

. . . and slide down it.

I wish we had snow on our planet.

Day 63
It was Earthling Daughter's birthday today.
What a party!

I think we should celebrate
these special days
on our planet.

However, I would not invite Earthling Dog. What a party animal!

Day 86

Every night, Earthling Mother reads us a bedtime story, tucks us in, and then kisses us good night.

I can't believe I look forward to this Earthling behavior. It makes me feel warm and fuzzy.

Fearless Leader, why don't we do bedtime stories on our planet?

Day 90

Earthling Daughter had her swim lesson today.

I didn't know that Earthlings float.

Unicorns don't.

Day 98

Earthling Daughter is sick today.

She sneezed and coughed all over me, but I don't mind.

Hugging me seems to make her feel better.

Day 99

Yep, she's all better!

I highly recommend hugs.

Day 100

My final report to you, Fearless Leader:

These Earthlings are a kind and loving family.

Their dog needs to learn to behave, but other than that, I really like it here.

So I'd say forget the invasion and send more of us to Earth for . . .

. . . a Unicorn Vacation!

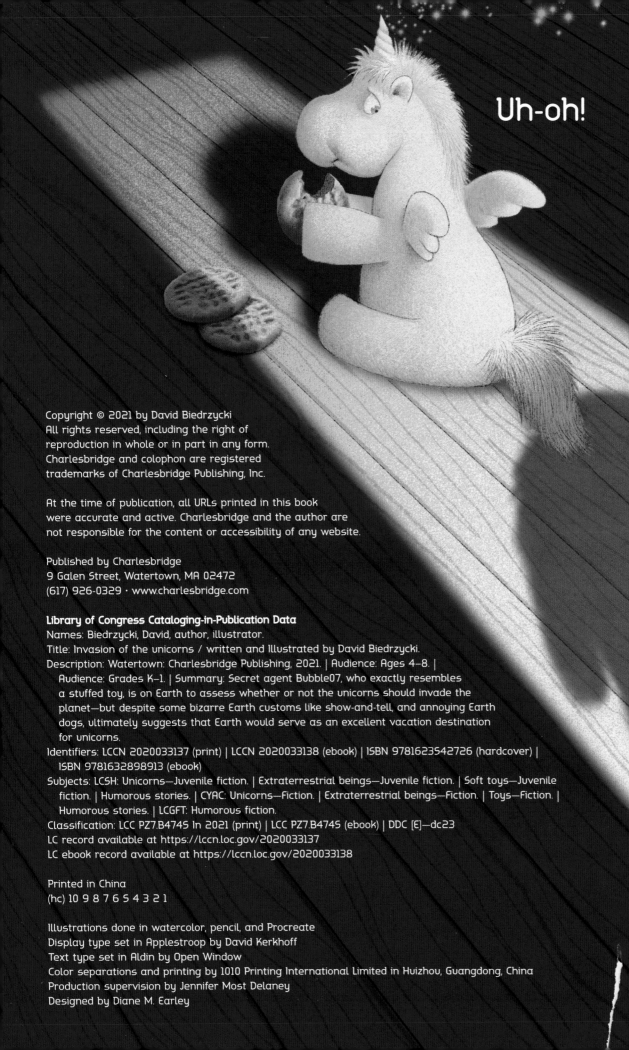

Uh-oh!

Copyright © 2021 by David Biedrzycki
All rights reserved, including the right of
reproduction in whole or in part in any form.
Charlesbridge and colophon are registered
trademarks of Charlesbridge Publishing, Inc.

At the time of publication, all URLs printed in this book
were accurate and active. Charlesbridge and the author are
not responsible for the content or accessibility of any website.

Published by Charlesbridge
9 Galen Street, Watertown, MA 02472
(617) 926-0329 · www.charlesbridge.com

Library of Congress Cataloging-in-Publication Data
Names: Biedrzycki, David, author, illustrator.
Title: Invasion of the unicorns / written and illustrated by David Biedrzycki.
Description: Watertown: Charlesbridge Publishing, 2021. | Audience: Ages 4–8. |
   Audience: Grades K–1. | Summary: Secret agent Bubble07, who exactly resembles
   a stuffed toy, is on Earth to assess whether or not the unicorns should invade the
   planet—but despite some bizarre Earth customs like show-and-tell, and annoying Earth
   dogs, ultimately suggests that Earth would serve as an excellent vacation destination
   for unicorns.
Identifiers: LCCN 2020033137 (print) | LCCN 2020033138 (ebook) | ISBN 9781623542726 (hardcover) |
   ISBN 9781632898913 (ebook)
Subjects: LCSH: Unicorns—Juvenile fiction. | Extraterrestrial beings—Juvenile fiction. | Soft toys—Juvenile
   fiction. | Humorous stories. | CYAC: Unicorns—Fiction. | Extraterrestrial beings—Fiction. | Toys—Fiction. |
   Humorous stories. | LCGFT: Humorous fiction.
Classification: LCC PZ7.B4745 In 2021 (print) | LCC PZ7.B4745 (ebook) | DDC [E]—dc23
LC record available at https://lccn.loc.gov/2020033137
LC ebook record available at https://lccn.loc.gov/2020033138

Printed in China
(hc) 10 9 8 7 6 5 4 3 2 1

Illustrations done in watercolor, pencil, and Procreate
Display type set in Applestroop by David Kerkhoff
Text type set in Aldin by Open Window
Color separations and printing by 1010 Printing International Limited in Huizhou, Guangdong, China
Production supervision by Jennifer Most Delaney
Designed by Diane M. Earley

*To my buddy Pete Wood,
who may have sold a toy unicorn or two.*

*Thanks to my neighbors
Amayah, Kirra, and Merryn DiNisco;
Jayden Mak; and Hailey Arnold.*

*Special thanks to Haileigh Hill
(aka Earthling Daughter). You got your wish!*